Measuring UP

Lily LaMotte ★ Ann Xu
Colors by Sunmi

HARPER alley

An Imprint of HarperCollinsPublishers

Chapter 1

In a small town in Taiwan...

My life in Taiwan is sweet.

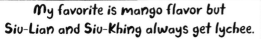

My favorite is mango flavor but Siu-Lian and Siu-Khing always get lychee.

We never get tired of watching the panda...

...or running on the Dragon Bridge...

...but A-má* is the best part.

*Grandmother

Every Saturday after A-má finishes her second cup of jasmine tea, we head to the morning market.

It's my favorite part of the weekend.

Mmmm.

sniff
sniff
sniff

The morning market smells like a candy store.

Bitter melon is healthy.*

*A-má only speaks in Taiwanese.

ha ha

Yuck!

I promise. You won't have to try it until you're ready.

A-má keeps her promises.

Cici, come help us get ready for our going-away party.

My parents decided to move to America.

I do NOT want to go.

6

Come visit for Moon Festival!

Lunar New Year!

Lantern Festival!

Children's Day!

I know!

You will finally be old enough to have a big birthday party!

I'll be seventy in a year.

That's forever!

A year is not that long.

Just as A-má made me a promise, I make a promise to myself that she will come for her birthday.

Maybe even sooner, if I keep asking her.

9

A long, long time ago

My grandmother...

...taught me.

We grind...

mash...

powder...

until...

My spices are the secret.

And now I teach it to you.

Are you going to teach Dad, too?

Aiyah! He has no interest. But you, Cici, you are always ready to learn and...

...part of me will go with you.

peppery AND minty

lemony AND flowery

I discover a whole new world of tastes.

But I am leaving my old world.

Will the food taste the same in Seattle? I try to memorize how it all tastes here.

CHOMP CHOMP

SLURP

mmmm mmm

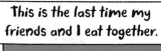

This is the last time my friends and I eat together.

mmmm mmmm

CHOMP CHOMP

SLURP

I even eat the bitter melon.

plop

plop

That's how I say goodbye. We leave the next day.

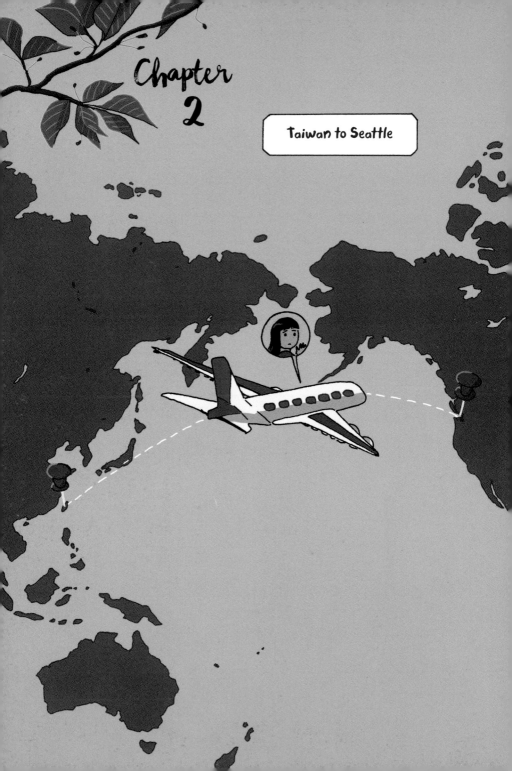

Chapter 2

Taiwan to Seattle

Chapter 3

First day of school

Welcome!

I was worried...

Jenna

...but I already made my first friend. It's going to be okay.

I'm so hungry and can't wait to dig into my own lunch.

She's got a fire going and it's not even for cooking!

Ci-ci? Jen-na is up-stairs. In my bed-room.

Emily, you know I've studied English in school since first grade?

I'm SO sorry. You weren't answering so I thought maybe...

It's okay. We all make mistakes.

I don't want to tell her I was too busy staring at her fireplace and thinking about the strangeness of Americans.

You don't know Sheila E.? She's only the best drummer. I'll show you some videos—

DING
DONG

gasp!

My parents are here.

You aren't going to sleep over?

Sleep here?

They told me of this strange American custom. It sounded like so much fun. I had to get Mom and Dad to let me stay.

Mom, Dad, it's a sleepover!

I had to explain it to them, too.

I don't think it's a good idea.

It's what American girls do. I want to stay. Please let me stay.

Good Taiwanese parents do not let their children do this.

But they're my new friends.

If you really want to do this, then yes. And I will stay with you tonight.

Emily, please may I speak to your mother—

Bye, Emily! Bye, Jenna! See you at school! Mom, Dad, come on!

I had to get my parents away before they embarrassed me.

I made friends at school, but I miss my old friends and . . .

Come for Lunar New Year.

A-má.

I ask her again to come. Even Dad tries.

Moon Festival.

Lantern Festival.

I'm so sorry.

I have to think of a way to bring A-má over. But I don't know how.

I can see why Sheila E. is Emily's hero.

That drummer sure can jam.

Chapter 4

The next day

Did you get the pineapple cakes I made?

Thank you, A-má! I always think of you when I eat them.

You don't have to thank me, Cici. Family doesn't need to thank each other.

clap clap clap

Guess what! I got 103 on my math test!

You are studying very hard. Don't forget to have fun.

You're so silly. I won't forget.

How are you? Moving to Seattle is a big change.

I have two best friends, Jenna and Emily. But...

I wish you would come visit.

29

Dad?

Hmm?

Are you happy we moved here?

I am. You will get a better education here. More opportunities. Remember—

Good grades, good college, good job, good life.

That is our family motto.

I think Dad misses A-má very much. I'm even more sure about surprising Dad.

Cici, I'm glad you got dinner started.

It's okay. It's kind of fun.

Chapter 6

Back to the present

I love eggs.

Want to trade desserts, too?

My grandmother's pineapple cake?

A-má's pineapple cake makes me think of her. And that reminds me that I need money for the plane ticket.

Okay, I can't say no to that look.

My friends try to help.

Sell some of your things.

My mom is always telling me to get rid of stuff.

RECYCLE LANDFILL COMPOST

Fun run fundraiser!

Friends gave my mom money for the marathon.

Find the approximate probability that a spinning penny will land heads up or that a paper cup will land down.

Poker tournament.

We do school car wash fundraisers all the time!

You could walk dogs.

I don't have one, or you could walk mine.

But they don't.

Sleepover at my house tomorrow night!

I got a new facial mask we can try out.

Maybe next time.

I haven't dared ask my parents about doing a sleepover again. Besides, I've got to figure out how to get the money.

I just don't know how.

Look!

Tsuí-kiáu
(dumpling)

Tshuah-ping
(shaved ice)

Bah-tsàng
(sticky rice dumpling
in banana leaf)

Lóo-bah-pn̄g
(minced pork
over rice)

...I only cook
Taiwanese foods.

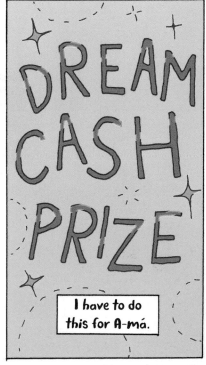

DREAM
CASH
PRIZE

I have to do
this for A-má.

This is your
answer! You're
going to win!

Yay, I'm
going to
win!

How much is the prize?

One...

thousand...

dollars.

That's enough to bring A-má!

Sign me up!

You're very lucky. You got the last spot.

Just bring back this parental consent form.

I will! Tomorrow.

There is only one small problem...

You've come to pray to your ancestors!

Mom, I...um—

Yeah, that's why I'm here.

We pray, then we eat.

It can't hurt to pray that Mom signs the consent form.

Please protect everybody's health and safety.

Please rest in peace.

Mom?

You're supposed to be praying.

A Happy Mom is a Say Yes Mom.

Want to hear a secret?

Don't tell DAD! A-má and I want to surprise him. She's coming for her birthday.

But how? I can't take money to buy a plane ticket without telling your dad. We send money to her every month, but even with that...And with the cut in her pension, I don't think she has—

I'll win the money to bring A-má here.

PRIZE MONEY
$ $

I tell her about the cooking contest... prize money... plane ticket.

All you have to do is sign this.

PLATINUM JR. CHEF PARENTAL CONSENT

I want to help A-má come in time for her birthday. A-má says it's bad luck if we celebrate after.

You're my good girl.

You know Dad will worry if your grades slip.

I'll keep my grades up.

Promise?

I promise.

It paid to pray, after all.

I start practicing for the contest by making dinner every night.

Your mother works very hard. You are a very good girl. So thoughtful to your mother.

Chapter 7

Saturday, two weeks later

ROUND 1

Time to go!

I can't decide. Red for success and good fortune or green for money and wealth?

Someone looks like a Christmas tree.

Too funny, Dad! Gotta go!

We need to get out fast before he asks where we're going.

Cici, you're all checked in. Relax, you'll be fine.

I check out the competition. They look like they're just as nervous. Except the girl next to me.

I don't know why she's such a grump.

I'm in so much trouble. How do I compete against someone with her own restaurant?

You have them all beat with your knife skills.

Twirl the pasta into a neat nest.

Don't pack ground meat.

It makes the meatball too dense and dry.

Yes, Dad.

We give each other the **Head Nod of Understanding**.

I brought your toque and knife roll.

Let's get started!

She even has her own knives! I'm burnt toast. I don't know why I thought I could win this for A-má.

47

Welcome to Platinum Jr. Chef, because platinum is obviously better than iron.

I'm Mr. Grant, owner of this store and head judge. Impress me and you could be on your way to winning the grand prize!!

Our other judges are—

You already know my right-hand man, er, should I say right-hand woman?

Ms. Kindling

And over here, we have local celebrity chef Mr. Bonze, owner of the esteemed Le Bec-Fin.

Mr. Bonze

That's right. A real chef will judge you.

Each week, I'll present you with a key ingredient that you must use in your dish.

Other than that, you can use any ingredient in the store and in the pantry.

Sadly, one team will be eliminated each round.

Teams! This may not be so bad if I get paired with Miranda of the Knives.

Ms. Kindling, what are the six teams?

I cross my fingers twice for double good luck.

48

I give you... rice.

I KNOW rice! I mean I REALLY know rice. I know rice better than anyone.

You have a few minutes to agree on your dish. No fighting, kids!

I know what I want to make.

My mom's minced pork over rice.

You mean complicated?

I mean is it fancy?

We can't win making Chinese food.

It's Taiwanese.

Is it sophisticated?

50

It's homey.

I want to make porcini risotto.

What's that?

It's Italian CUISINE. Rice cooked with porcini and broth. Then I add Parmigiano-Reggiano.

You won't be able to stop eating it.

Yes, let's do it!

ha

ha

ha

Her risotto sounds like an Italian version of Mom's muê.* She's making Taiwanese food.

*rice porridge

Dried porcini

Voilà!

My partner isn't just an expert—

Miranda is a **MAGICIAN**.

But I still know how to wash rice.

I'll wash the rice.

It's not laundry.

But I always wash rice.

Wash rice? Why would you do that? You'll wash away the starch that makes risotto creamy.

Oh.

I thought I knew rice—but I'm wrong.

FRESH
porcini

Stirring

Parmigiano-
Reggiano

Stirring

Sage

Stirring

It's only thirty minutes. You're not tired, are you?

Who? Me? No!

For A-má, I will stir into the night if I have to.

Judging Round 1

Hmm, your Thai green curry has something missing.

Even if it is missing something, it smells yummy. Maybe I can get my parents to try Thai food.

Refreshing! Nothing like a little citrus to wake the palate.

Citrus rice salad

A taste of New Orleans, or as I like to call it, Nawlins.

Hmmph. Flavor profile is okay.

Red beans and rice

Everyone's food looks so yummy. I don't know who they're going to let go.

I love rice pudding. It reminds me of warm pudding on cold mornings after Christmas Day when I was a child.

I don't know if we can compete against Christmas memories.

I can't tell if the judges like the frittata with rice and asparagus.

Then *it* is our turn.

Somehow the walk to the judges takes forever.

And then *in* a split second, ready or *not*, we're there.

hmmph

He hates it. I just know it.

I TOLD YOU SO

I can put up with her attitude for five more Saturdays. I'm doing this for my family.

Excellent, excellent. The rice is perfect.

Well done.

You all made delicious dishes. I don't know who the grand prize winner will be except... my growing belly.

After much deliberation, we have decided to call down...

Christopher and Adam.

Your Thai green curry did not make the cut.

Miranda and I did it. We're a team!

I told you we shouldn't make your Thai food.

Team? Ha! We're just working together.

Taiwanese, not Thai.

My bad.

Miranda doesn't know everything. But maybe she was right about not making Asian food.

Chapter 8

Good morning, good night, my winning girl.

SIZZLE

I believe in you, Cici.

You do?

Let me show you.

I bought new luggage at the morning market.

She had so much faith in me...

The morning market isn't the same without you.

But I will come soon and you'll show me the big Pike Place Market.

When do you compete again?

Every Saturday. There were twelve of us but we're down to ten. With eliminating a team each round, there will be five more rounds. The last one is the finals.

I'll think of you every Saturday.

Now it's bedtime for me. Have a good day at school.

I WON'T let her down.

I know you like eggs.

Mom, you're the best.

You don't know anything. Cici isn't cooking Chinese.

Mmm, I love orange chicken.

She cooks American. So there.

That's right. American!

I wish they didn't assume that I'm cooking American. Besides...

I'm Taiwanese, not Chinese.

No one hears me.

Chapter 9

ROUND 2

I've got Miranda, but is she enough?

We're going to win this.

Um, I hope we got this.

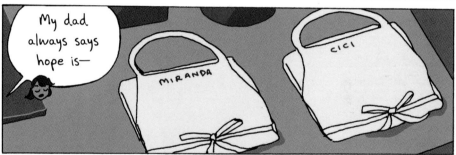

My dad always says hope is—

MIRANDA

CICI

snap

a dull blade.

I think her family motto just took mine to the mat.

GRADES COLLEGE JOB LIFE

I have reached the end of my Italian pasta knowledge.

I help Miranda gather
the rest of the ingredients.

olive
oil

ground
beef

Parmigiano-
Reggiano
cheese

butter

pepper

tomato
paste

salt

onion

tomatoes

carrot

celery

milk

My heart thumps
in nervous time.

I'll chop onions and you brown the meat.

You're like a samurai.

With a lot of practice, I could work the knife like her.

A LOT of practice.

But now I'm just browning the meat and...

...boiling the pasta. **No-brainer.**

Make it al dente.

I've got it. I cook noodles all the time.

I almost ask her what she means, but then she'd keep treating me as if I don't know anything. I do know things...

A-má used chicken liver to give deeper flavor.

I have to hurry to the next step—the sauce.

We don't have time to cook the ragu all day. The electric pressure cooker will speed things up.

FWEE EE E!

You're not scared, are you?

Me? No!

I've used one plenty of times. My dad says I'll run the restaurant one day.

oh~

Miranda is so lucky. She already knows she'll be a chef. I still have no clue what I'll be one day.

We're ahead of schedule. Time to drain the noodles.

tick

tick

tick

Let me taste the pasta.

I'll show Miranda she's not the only one who can cook.

I can't serve the judges this overcooked mush. I will cook new pasta.

Go! Go! I'll get more pasta.

I'm sorry. I'll fill the pot.

You overcooked the pasta! It's not al dente.

I cooked it just like at home.

I didn't want to look stupid by asking earlier, but here I am.

Hurry...

Do you have the water heated up yet?

Hurry...

So slow!

A watched pot never boils... and a watched pot never fills.

I got you, A-má.

What did you say?

Um, I'm heating the water.

Don't forget to salt the water.

That's strange. We never salt the water at home.

Ugh, no more bucatini!

Don't panic, Miranda. I can use radiatore.

It looks like an accordion.

Look at the time!

I messed up bad.

Oh no! We need time to cook the pasta. Then we still have to sauce and plate it.

We're racing against the clock as it ticks down.

BZZZZZZZ

Let's see how you've transformed the ingredient. Ms. Kindling, who will be the first team?

Cici and Miranda, please bring up your dish.

The sauce is delicious. Wonderful choice to make spaghetti sauce... or should I say radiatore sauce. Eh?

Ooo
Ooo

Just the right acidity balanced with the sweetness.

I detect a touch of chicken liver.

Chicken liver?!

It gives minerality. Elevates the complexity of the ragu.

Oh!

I won't mention any names, but someone (not me) was wrong about the chicken livers.

Yum, there's something magical about tomatoes and cumin. And pie. Pie is magical even if it's not apple pie.

Todd & Jacob's tamale pie

I detect a hint of bean slime. Next time rinse your canned beans.

I try to be patient as we wait for the others to be judged.

I didn't know about bean slime. I wouldn't have done any better than Todd and Jacob.

What's this? I love surprises.

Creative use of smoked mozzarella, but—

How delightful! It's like a Swedish Thanksgiving.

Mark & Rose's Swedish meatballs with cranberry sauce

Robert & Samantha's mozzarella stuffed meatloaf

Yes, interesting concept.

Mr. Bonze always has a "but." I wouldn't want to be his kid. At least Mom and Dad have "and."

The judges like it, I think. Only one more dish for judging and I still can't tell if we're making it to the next round.

Complexity of spices. I taste cumin, coriander, cayenne, our very own chili powder. Be sure to tell your moms about our wonderful chili powder.

Layla & Crystal's calico bean chili

Did you know that in Texas, beans are taboo?

That's so interesting, but I'm more interested in...did we make it to the next round?!

...allspice.

We didn't use allspice!

We did it!

YIPPEE!

You were right about the chicken liver.

Dad put in a stellar kitchen with anything we could want. Unless you want to do it at your house?

NO! I mean, your house has all the equipment. Let's do it there.

Want to come to my house? You know, just to get some practice... and work better as a team.

Miranda thinks we're a team! Team Cici-Miranda. Or Team Ci-randa. Can I get her to go for that? Nah.

I never bring my friends home. They won't understand the way we live.

82

Chapter 10

Next afternoon, Sunday

Can I go?

Who will be there? Is her mom or dad home? Who is supervising?

She said there will be adult supervision.

It's like the sleepover at **Emily**'s house. I don't know why **Mom** is being so protective.

Miranda asked me to her house. We're going to prep for the next round.

I'm glad you made another friend.

If I let you go, you'll come home right after. No wandering off.

I promise.

I wait for Mom to decide.

Go ask Dad.

But—

You can do it if Dad says yes.

I go right away to ask Dad.

But first, I get my secret weapon, which I'm sure will persuade Dad to let me go.

I explain to Dad that I need to go to my friend's house.

pant
pant

I got a 100 percent on my test! So I can go!

Did you ask your mom?

She said yes.

Obviously that's what she meant when she asked me to ask Dad.

Okay, go ahead.

I'll call to let her know right now.

Before Dad changes his mind.

The next day after school...

=BEEP= =BEEP=

Thanks for giving me a ride, Mrs....

Miss Amy Jones. She's been taking care of me since I was but a wee bairn.

I'm not Scottish. Miranda just likes her games. I'm English.

You have your own Mary Poppins!

Amy is my second mom. My mom travels a lot.

I hear you two are quite the team.

We're pretty good together.

Miranda told Amy we're a team! Should I give Team Mi-ci a try?

Nah.

85

What made you enter the contest, Cici?

I'm using the prize money to surprise my dad with my grandmother's visit. She's turning seventy years old.

Mom and Dad talk about getting her a green card so she can live with us. But...

It takes years. I'm still in the queue for mine.

I didn't know that. You never told me.

You need a green card? But you're...

Yes, English. It wouldn't matter if I were German, French, Italian, Australian. We all have to get one.

I thought we were the only ones who need green cards. I learned something new.

Yeah, it's okay...

I like having my own bathroom.

You're so lucky.

Mom wouldn't like cleaning the extra bathroom. Dad would say it's a waste.

Hmm, you're right. I am lucky that way.

Mom's paintings.

They're so beautiful.

She's the artistic one in the family.

Let's cook!

It's like her kitchen swallowed the cooking store!

I wish I had even one of these gadgets.

Waste of money. Only need cleaver.

I know Mom is right, but still.

You have enough food to last through a zombie apocalypse.

Dad would whip up a dish to distract them.

I've never seen so many spices.

Dad likes to experiment, cooking up new dishes for the restaurant.

I've never been so jealous.

She has so many spices I've never heard of.

You're so lucky.

Yeah, sure.

Want to start with spices? Close your eyes and try to guess what it is.

I'm game!

I think it's salt. But it's flaky and crunchy.

It's Fiore di Cervia. It's a finishing salt you sprinkle on top of your food.

Salt isn't just boring salt! I have so much to learn.

You get half a point.

We don't have to keep track.

slide

Okay, but it won't be as much fun.

I KNOW this taste.

My grandmother uses cardamom.

Mom makes Finnish cardamom bread every Christmas.

That sounds so special.

I wake up extra early so I get the first slice.

Next spice is...

Oh! You use it, too!

It's warm, a little spicy, and smoky, but I don't know what it is.

Ding! Sorry, contestant.

What is it?

Espelette. A pepper from Basque country. Want to try another?

I want to taste more.

So many spices I've never tried.

There are too many to do them all. Taste these and then I'll quiz you.

Tasting spice is thirsty work. Let's see how many I get right in one minute.

My dad is one, too. A lot of chefs are.

You're still great! You got us through the rounds. And someday you're going to run your dad's restaurant.

I'm not.

Can I tell you a secret?

Cooking isn't my thing. It's my dad's.

What do you want to be?

An artist like Mom. Sort of. I make comic books.

Is that even a thing?

Yes! Someone has to write and draw them. Why not me?

I never thought about it before.

My dad would ground me until I'm old like him.

It's going to be hard telling your dad.

Yeah.

Can I see your comic book?

You want to see it? Okay!

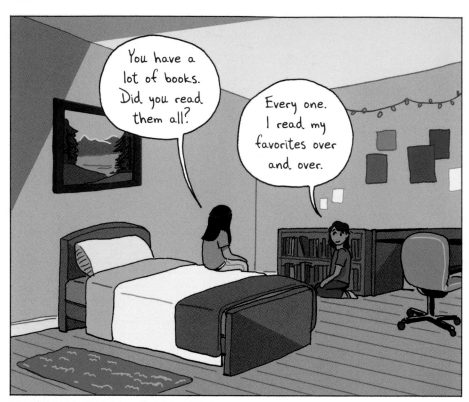

You have a lot of books. Did you read them all?

Every one. I read my favorites over and over.

You can have this one.

YANG / AMERICAN CHINESE

"Genius" Yang is awesome. You'll totally get it because you're Chinese.

Taiwanese.

Yes, Taiwanese.

But I will get it.

I'll show you the comic book I'm writing if you promise not to tell.

Hmm mmmmmm

zipp!

I know it's just a silly—

ha ha ha

I like it! Goats don't wear capes and a mask and fly like Superman. And he's trying to get his goatee out of his eyes. He's so silly and funny.

Thanks, Cici. You're the best.

Now you're silly.

Yeah, I didn't know what to do with her praise.

Chapter 11

ROUND 3

Secret ingredient: zucchini

We'll make chocolate chocolate chip cookies.

You can't make cookies from veggies.

You'll see. Trust me.

flour

salt

baking powder

cocoa

sugar

butter

eggs

zucchini

vanilla

chocolate chips

I hope Miranda knows what she's doing.

We'll cream the butter and sugar together until it's fluffy.

Why is it butter and sugar smell so delicious together?

Go ahead and mix the flour, cocoa powder, baking powder, and salt together in a bowl.

We'll mix this up, then put in the dry ingredients.

What about eggs? Shouldn't they go in?

I like to put them in last so I can taste the batter and make sure it's right.

Not bad, huh?

Not bad but...

You're right. It's missing something.

I've got an idea. Wait here!

Bay leaf, bouquet garni, caraway... and then I find it.

I know exactly what we need to add.

We can sprinkle it on top of the cookies.

Maybe. I'll bake up a couple of samples.

You WERE right! I can't stop eating these.

I know I shouldn't be so happy that she approves.

I am the supertaster, after all. But still it feels good.

Layla and Crystal. You brought home the bacon on the zucchini fries.

Your dish is a kid pleaser. Kudos on that.

But a bit uninspired.

I feel bad for Layla and Crystal. I bet the kids in school would gobble them up.

Todd and Jacob, your zucchini cake is moist, and the addition of walnuts adds a nice crunch.

The cream cheese frosting gives it a nice tang to contrast with the sweetness of the cake.

Tsk, tsk. I see you ran out of time to bake your cake. The middle is inedible.

Robert and Samantha, your scrambled eggs with grated zucchini is a nice variation on regular scrambles. Nicely done.

I really liked the lightness of the eggs.

Hmm, a bit runny. Next time you should squeeze more moisture out of the zucchini. I hope the last team does better.

Todd and Jacob. Despite the deliciousness of your cake, I'm afraid not baking your cake until done eliminates you.

We make it through. But I feel bad for Todd and Jacob.

We did it! We make such an awesome team.

We do!

I'm glad they put us together.

Okay, everyone. You know how much I like surprises.

We have one for you.

No!

Shhh. I can't hear.

I do **NOT** like surprises. Mom and Dad surprised me with the move to Seattle. Surprises make my stomach jiggle.

Since we are down to the last six contestants, you will no longer work as teams.

GROAN

Oh no!

Don't mess with our success.

But we like working in teams!

How am I going to get through the next round without Miranda?

Even worse! Now I'm competing against her.

I can see that some of you are upset. But with this change, we are also going to give you the ingredient for next week.

This way, you can practice your best dishes with the ingredient.

And since you have an entire week to practice, we expect even better things from you. So next week's ingredient is...

I give you... potatoes!

We don't eat potatoes at home. I am in trouble. Big trouble. I need to start practicing right away!

Chapter 12

The next day

I need to wow the judges and that means research at the library for the best potato recipes.

tak tak tak tak tak

Can you take me to the library? Please?

Now? Can't it wait? I've got a production problem at work.

But I have to STUDY for the cooking contest.

tak tak tak

"Study" is a magic word around here. It always works . . .

Don't you dare crash! Not now!

. . . except this time. I guess production problems are serious.

I need to do RESEARCH. Can you drive me to the library?

"Research" is the other magic word around here.

I have a deadline at work. Ask Mom.

But not this time.

I am not giving up on A-má. I'll walk there. I won't melt.

Ms. Green is my favorite librarian. She knows EVERYTHING.

Cici, how wonderful that you're doing a cooking contest. I'm so happy that cooking isn't a lost art among you young folks.

I need a how-to-cook-American cookbook. The best one you have.

Julia Child
Mastering the Art of French Cooking

I have something even better.

I need an AMERICAN cookbook.

Oh, I heard you the first time.

But it's French.

DVDS

Julia Child taught American housewives how to cook in the '60s. She even had her own cooking show.

Take a look at this.

The French Chef

Trust me on this one. You want Julia Child.

Thanks, Ms. Green.

I knew Ms. Green would come through for me. And then I had another idea.

Can I ask you a question about comics?

I'm still wondering what Julia Child can do for me when I see a restaurant that looks familiar but don't know why. We never eat out because "Why waste money when we cook?"

Then I realize...

This is perfect! I can see Miranda right now.

I'm sorry. We're not open yet.

Is Miranda here?

I'm Cici. From the cooking contest.

So YOU'RE her new friend!

I'll go get her.

We're testing a new pasta recipe—lemon.

Can I help?

It's boring.

How can this be boring?

Did you come just to see me?

Yes...no. I was at the library and was walking home a different way and saw this place and...

Oh boy, I am not making any sense.

ha ha ha

At least you're honest.

I've never made pasta. Would you show me?

You can help me knead.

This place is so cool.

I guess so. I've been working here since I could walk.

Really?

Almost. Use the heel of your hand to knead a little harder.

It used to be exciting.

Miranda's so lucky. I wish I was the one to take over the restaurant.

Good grades, good college, good job, good life.

Miranda doesn't look like she thinks she's lucky, though.

What's wrong?

Amy's going back to England.

You'll miss her.

But she'll be back soon?

No, she's getting married and not coming back. She says I'm too old for a nanny.

I'm sorry. I miss my grandmother so I know what it's like.

Did you have a nanny, too?

My grandmother took care of me. But now I look after myself.

Amy is right! I'm too old for a nanny.

But she's not just your nanny.

I know what'll make her happy.

pat pat

Miranda, I have—

Who do we have here?

You saw her at the first round. She was my partner.

Yes, that's right.

Here to do a little spying?

DAD!

You decided to show her how to make our special pasta?

Er, no. She asked.

A couple of times.

I waited for Miranda to tell her dad that I wasn't spying.

I wasn't spying. I don't need your recipes.

I speed out of there as fast as I can. I'll show them what I can do.

I don't understand how Julia Child can help me...

Get your butter hot, then just put the potatoes in.

You can sauté these... or you can bake them. I think it's rather fun just to do it this way.

...but as I watch show after show...

...I fall under her spell.

I'm going to try and flip this over, which is a daring thing to do.

When you flip anything, you really must have the courage of your conviction.

...courage of conviction...

Courage of Conviction.

COURAGE
CONVICTION

I know then what I need to beat Miranda and the others.

See, when I flipped it, I didn't have the courage to do it the way I should have.

Julia flubs her flip. On TV! She is in so much trouble.

But you can always pick it up...who is going to see?

Everyone would see she's not perfect.

She doesn't care.

But the only way to learn how to flip things is to just flip them.

The only way to flip things is to just flip them.

She's like my American A-má. She even speaks English with a strange accent.

119

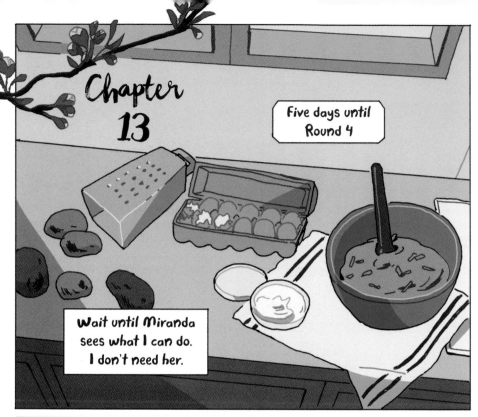

Chapter 13

Five days until Round 4

Wait until Miranda sees what I can do. I don't need her.

I just need to watch Julia again...

And again.

And try again.

I can do this. I just need Julia's courage of conviction.

But even that isn't enough. This is so much harder than studying for a test. And a lot messier.

What is going on here?!

Hi, Dad. Let me explain.

So I confess.

You've been going to a cooking contest so you can buy a plane ticket so A-má can come here for her seventieth birthday and...

surprise me?

That's the plan?

Aiyah, I don't know what to say.

You could be better than me. You see that, right? Promise me you will get good grades.

It isn't worth a few days of celebration for something that could affect the rest of your life.

But it is important that you spend your time studying. You could eventually be the head of a research lab.

Promise.

Now go study. I'll clean this up.

But even as I work through the math, I wonder if I want what Dad wants for me.

I spend the rest of the week studying for a test and trying to practice more cooking, but I'm running out of time.

What are you making? Have you eaten?

Tomorrow is the next round. I've failed again to make Julia's recipe.

Not yet.

Potato pancakes. But I keep messing them up.

It looks... edible.

Can you help me?

I want to help, but...

It's okay.

I still don't know how to make American food.

See this? Americans didn't know how to cook until she taught them. Now she can teach you.

Julia Child

Mastering the Art of French Cooking

In that case, we'll make potato pancakes for dinner.

One more try at potato pancakes, but this time...

...I have a teammate.

I'm surprised Dad hasn't said anything about all the potato pancakes we've been eating this week.

I have to confess that Dad knows about the surprise.

He didn't even let on. He knows how to keep a secret himself.

Not that one. We need curved sides.

Head slap!

And then comes the all-important step...

Chapter 14

Six contestants

Hey.

Hey.

Umm...

Surprise ingredient: sweet potato

Taiwan is shaped like a sweet potato. This is a sign.

I don't need her help. I can make my dish all by myself.

...the ingredient for the semifinals.

In the right hands, or should I say, the right can, this ingredient has taken down bullies.

Spinach

Get it? Like in Popeye? Ha ha!

Who is Popeye?

Ewww

So we have a moment.

Doesn't mean anything.

Chapter 15

The next morning, Sunday

When I come, I will give you the biggest hug. Prepare to be squeezed. And I want to meet your friends. Jenna and Emiry.

Em-i-ly.

That's what I said. Em-i-ry.

You have to see Emily's house. They have a fireplace. They actually build a fire inside their house.

Okay, it is very late here. Hó-ūn.* I know you will do well in the next round.

I hear American houses are all made of wood. Aiyah! Burning a fire inside!

*Good luck

After we hang up, I look through Julia's cookbook.

I turn to the spinach section and look for a recipe that'll get me through the semifinals.

Blanched, chopped spinach will get me chopped from the contest.

Puree of spinach isn't much better.

Spinach with butter or cream. Add some chopped ham. Creamy but not exciting enough.

Wow! Spinach and cheese three ways: gratinéed, canapés, and cheese sauce.

Julia sure likes her spinach and cheese combos.

And then I see what I need...

This time I'll be the one to surprise the judges.

Chapter 16

Final four

ROUND 5

No Miranda meeting me at the door this time. It feels a little lonely for some reason. But I quickly brush it off. I have a contest to win.

Hey.

Hey.

Ummm... I want to tell you—

CLAP
CLAP
CLAP
CLAP
CLAP

The four of you have risen to the top like cream.

I am proud of all of you for making it this far. You have done wonderfully.

You're all decent cooks, so this round of competition will be the hardest one yet.

Mr. Grant likes surprises. I have the perfect dish: Julia's Spinach Surprise. Or should I say Julia and Cici's Spinach Surprise because I'm putting my own twist on it.

milk

flour

whipping cream

butter

spinach

eggs

salt

nutmeg

cheddar cheese*

cinnamon**

*Swiss is holey,^ but cheddar is better.
**I'm adding cinnamon since everything is better with it. But that's just my opinion.
^pun intended

I dunk the spinach into water to blanch it. That's a word I learned from Julia.

Then I dunk the spinach into the ice water to refresh it. Blanching and icing keeps vegetables fresh instead of turning into the goop at the school cafeteria.

Squeeze the water out of the spinach.

Then chop, chop, chop.

Finally, after all that, I sauté the spinach in butter and a pinch of nutmeg and cinnamon.

A little flour, a little stir.

A glug of cream and a bit of cheese, please.

Butter, cream, and cheese is magical. It even works on spinach.

Now to make the surprise of Julia's Spinach Surprise.

Voilà! My surprise is ready.

Polenta pizza with spinach and pancetta

mmm

This is a charming take on the Northern Italian staple.

Miranda's so creative. She'll make it to the finals, leaving one less spot for me to make it.

No, just no. The yolk is hard.

Layla's spinach salad with fried egg

I feel bad for Layla.

Non tutte le ciambelle riescono col buco.

Is that Italian?!

I speak Italian with Nonna and Nonno. It's Nonna's favorite Italian saying. It says that not all doughnuts come out with a hole.

She does it, too—talks to her grandmother in another language...

Still doesn't make us friends.

Next dish, please.

I can't tell what Samantha made.

What did you make?

You eat bread with a spoon?

Spinach spoon bread from my gramma's recipe.

It's more like a pudding.

Mr. Bonze does **NOT** look amused. Please don't tell me I messed up my chances.

I have a surprise to announce before we tell you the results.

The judges have a surprise.

Mr. Bonze looks happy. It'll be bad.

You are all wonderful but we must quickly come to a close.

Like last round, we'll eliminate two of you again.

That means there will be only two finalists. Not only that, but we're giving you two weeks to prepare.

But we giveth and we taketh. So I'm not revealing the ingredient.

Ha-ha! Don't you just love surprises?

But...but how will I study for this? It's worse than a pop quiz.

One of the finalists going into the final round is...

Miranda.

I am sorry. Layla, you have been eliminated.

You're a good egg, but you're overcooked.

Anybody can overcook eggs.

It's so easy to do.

Keep cooking. You're great.

And now. The moment you've all been waiting for.

I'm pulling for you.

And the other finalist is...

Cici!

I did it. I made it to the finals.

FI-NALS FI-NALS FI-NALS FI-NALS

Chapter 17

grrr grrr

Two weeks until the final round

I'll make some for you, too.

American food again? Can you make rice, too? You know how Mom loves her rice.

Did you study for your math test?

I want you to study.

We had a math test.

Study for your *NEXT* test, then.

There's always another test. It's the definition of school.

Dad doesn't understand, but I can always count on A-má.

Remember that tests make you better and stronger up here.

Yes, Dad.

My mother and father worked from sunup to sundown. It was a very hard life for them. A-kong* worked very hard, too, right up until the day he died.

My life was easier because I taught in the high school. And your mother and father's lives are even better. Your father wants you to be more successful.

*Grandfather

But I need to study Julia. I can really cook.

It does not matter if I come now, if you throw away your future.

But it's bad luck to celebrate after your birthday.

We can't miss her birthday and... more important, I miss her soft hugs.

What is important is that you keep doing well in school. That you have a good future.

You sound like Dad.

Cici, you need to listen to your father.

Yes, A-má.

I can't believe A-má didn't come through for me. After making potato pancakes with me, it feels like Mom understands me more.

So I keep cooking dinners. Dad still wants rice and when Mom gets home from work, we make dinner together. I even teach Mom a new cucumber dish.

Baked cucumbers

Chocolate and almond cake

You're not making junk food, are you?

Cheese puffs

And with a test coming, I try to study as much as I normally would.

Too quickly, it's the end of the week and the day of the math test.

But maybe I haven't studied enough.

I'm 99.99 percent sure that Dad is not going to be happy. Maybe I shouldn't have spent all that time cooking.

It has to be worth it. We will all be together like we used to be.

Chapter 18

I have another week, but it doesn't feel like enough time to get ready.

Want to come over? Emily and I are going to play *Civilization*. We're trying to figure out how to save the planet from CLIMATE CHANGE!

I can't. I have to practice for the cooking contest.

We never see you anymore after school.

Can we help you practice?

You want to?

Let us help!

We want to do it!

They are my friends, so I don't know why I'm so surprised.

I have a terrifying idea.

146

My house doesn't look anything like theirs or the ones on TV.

I race ahead as if I can outrun my invitation.

They're my friends. They won't do a "rotten worm" scene when they see how I live.

Maybe we shouldn't do it today.

Why not?

I need time to get ready.

When my mom thinks our house is too messy for anyone to come over, she says the same thing. We don't care. My room is always a mess.

My parents aren't home.

Your parents won't care. We're not strangers.

No stranger danger from us.

What if for the first time, they really realize how Taiwanese I am? What if they stop seeing me as being like them?

If they laugh I'll...

...I'll lose my best friends.

CLK

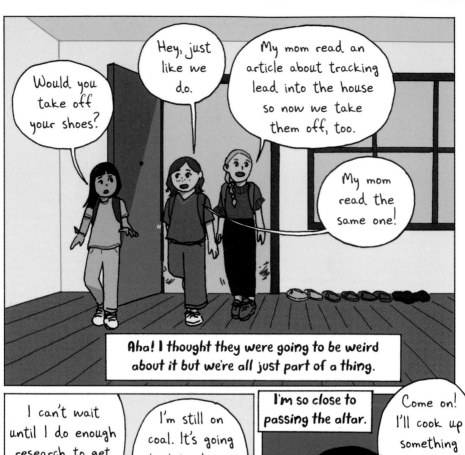

Would you take off your shoes?

Hey, just like we do.

My mom read an article about tracking lead into the house so now we take them off, too.

My mom read the same one!

Aha! I thought they were going to be weird about it but we're all just part of a thing.

I can't wait until I do enough research to get geothermal or a wind farm.

I'm still on coal. It's going to take hours of play to get better tech.

Ha ha, I finally realize they're talking about their video game. Maybe I can get them past the altar before they notice it.

I'm so close to passing the altar.

Come on! I'll cook up something that'll wow you.

And Mom bought ice cream, too.

I think I'm in the clear. And then . . .

Are they your grandparents?

They're my mom's parents and my dad's father.

Mom likes to...

•••

That's spiritual rice. Even when you've moved on, you still have to eat. Right?

I know! It's like when we go to the cemetery every year and light candles for our grandparents. It's an Irish thing.

I didn't know the Irish do that.

My mom keeps her dad on our mantelpiece.

That can't be...

She keeps his ashes in a fancy urn.

I saw the urn at her house but had no idea.

When I was little, I worried his ashes would creep out at night.

Not that I'm still scared or anything.

152

You promised us eats.

Coming!

But first I better leave a message for Mom so she knows what I'm doing.

Mom, my best friends, Jenna and Emily, are over and we, um, I mean me, I, so I'm going to make them a snack. I hope it's okay. I promise not to do anything I shouldn't. We'll be very g—

-BEEP-

I guess my voice mail was just a tiny bit long. And now to make snacks.

I'm so ready to show them.

flour

eggs

swiss cheese

nutmeg

salt & pepper

butter

I made cheese puffs. What do you think?

Yum!

Yummo!

Caramel custard

Chocolate and almond cake

This is so good. But your grandmother's pineapple cake is still the best.

I always thought she just likes dessert. But she likes A-má's Taiwanese dessert more! Hmm...

How did you learn to make all this?

Thanks for being my taste testers.

It's about time you asked us over.

Julia says you can make anything. You just need Courage of Conviction.

Courage of Conviction! Courage of Conviction!

I was worried my friends would find my house weird. I like having them over.

Everyone did well on the test.

YES!

Not bad.

They're so happy with their grades. Dad would kill me.

Cici, please stay after class.

I've never been asked to stay after class before.

I'm just not a math person. Not like her.

Grrr, I study hard for my grades. Usually.

Are things okay with you?

I think so.

You've gotten 100 percent on every test this year. Until now.

Sometimes even a kid like you needs a little help. Everyone does. It's okay.

I worked hard not to fail Mom, Dad, and A-má.

I'd be happy to work with you after school if you like.

Don't worry about this one grade. There will be more tests.

Don't worry?! She has no idea. I don't know how I'm going to tell Dad.

I just know Dad will find out, but I won't think of it right now.

splash   splash

Szz z z z z

chop chop   chop chop

BOO—UP
BOO—UP

I forgot to call A-má!

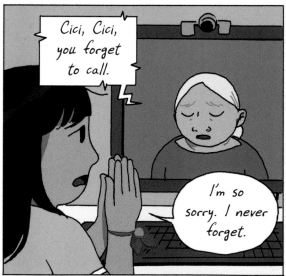

Cici, Cici, you forget to call.

I'm so sorry. I never forget.

Aiyah, I can never stay mad at you.

You are an excellent chef. You will win.

You haven't tasted the food I've been making.

I can smell your cooking all the way from here.

You're silly.

I am proud, very proud.

You're a lucky girl. But better than luck, you'll always be successful because you work hard.

I...
I do.

I don't know what to be more angry about...

Um, you could not be angry?

Okay, maybe not the best choice.

Sorry, Dad.

You did poorly on the test. Even worse, you lied to me.

I'm so sorry.

I'll get an A on every test from now on. I promise. I won't lie to you again.

But—

I know you'll do better in school because you will quit the cooking contest.

Go to your room. You have a lot of studying to do.

Why? Why is it always good grades, good college, good job?

Having a good job is the only way to have a life where you aren't working as hard as our family has had to in the past.

My friends get Bs on their tests and their parents are happy.

Cici, they are American. They don't have to try as hard. When people see us, no matter how American we become, they always see someone who's not like them. We always have to prove ourselves first.

Is he right?

Then I know
what to say.

Chapter 20

Cici vs Miranda

This is the last time I will spend my Saturday cooking in the contest. Part of me is sad that it's ending.

FINALS!

They came to see you?

They're my friends.

I told them about it, but I didn't think...

COURAGE

You got this!

I didn't think they would come because...

We love your food!

...I still hadn't believed in them.

They actually believe in me. Dad might be right that I'll always have to prove myself first. But I have my friends and that's enough for now.

CICI! CICI! CIC

CICI! CICI!

I don't feel weird. I...

...feel...

...content.

Cici is changing.

It's good.

Yes... it is.

Good luck, Cici.

Thanks, Amy. I hear you're moving back to England.

I remember my own goodbye with A-má.

This is my fiancé, George. I wish...

You don't need me anymore. I know you'll be fine.

I...I...I want you to be happy.

I will be. And you will come visit. Anytime you want to talk, I'll be there for you.

Cici, I'm so sorry about my dad. I knew as soon as you left I should've stood up for you.

He messes with my head sometimes.

And I did feel okay. I know what it is like to have a dad telling me things that mess with my head. I do **NOT** want to be the head of a lab.

It's okay.

I brought the book with me because I had started to forgive her after the last round. And although I'm not sure we're real friends, I may not see her again after the contest is over.

What's this?

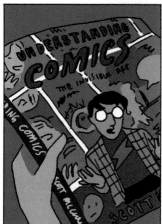

UNDERSTANDING COMICS

THE INVISIBLE ART

SCOTT

I bought it at the library. I'm sorry it's used.

I'm so glad I know you.

Final countdown

Chapter *sweet rice* 21

sweet rice

Iû-pñg* is celebration and...comfort.

shrimp

peanuts

mushrooms

pork tenderloin

scallions

soy sauce

sesame oil

salt

cardamom

*Oil rice is named for its greasy goodness.

I have a part of A-má in me and...

183

...I'm making the cardamom mine, too.

It's not just about A-má's birthday...

...and bringing her and Dad together.

I realize...

...it's more than that.

I want her to come share my new life and . . .

. . . I realize something even bigger.

I belong *here*—cooking rice for dinner so when Mom and Dad get home, the rice is done. Cooking for my friends and showing them a taste of Taiwan.

Now it is time to bring A-má here with her special dish.

I thought making A-má's dish would be enough, but even though it tastes like her food...

...something is missing.

Hey, I know you!

I have a new idea.

I think this is it. The lavender will work together with the cardamom to make a new complex flavor.

Courage of conviction...

I am made of A-má...

...and Julia.

Time!

Miranda and Cici, please bring your dishes up.

It's the moment of truth.

What did Miranda make? I didn't even peek.

It looks amazing. I don't know if I can beat that.

Please show us your best dish, Miranda.

You can do this.

She's still my friend.

And what did you bake for us?

It's a pistachio cardamom olive oil cake with cardamom buttercream and chopped pistachio sprinkled on top. I make it every year for my mother's birthday.

Such an unusual choice.

The combination of cardamom and pistachio works.

This is absolutely delicious.

But I don't want to lose either.

192

tak
tak
tak

Both dishes were winners.

WIN
WIN
WIN

Could it possibly be true...?

CICI

MIRANDA

But there can only be one winner.

I thought Mr. Bonze was the mean one!

Both your dishes are delicious. Miranda, your use of cardamom and pistachio complemented and brought out the best in each other. Cici, your yooo-bung is new to me, but it made me think of hearth and home with a snap of snazziness.

But did you infuse your soul into it?

A-má's soul.

Julia's soul.

My soul.

Who won?!

194

You must show Á-má your new cooking skills when she comes.

Cici, I want you to make the food for her birthday party.

I'll make Cici. With a little Julia Child.

And would you teach me your recipe?

I'll give you a lesson this week!

It's a deal.

198

She can use my sleeping bag.

That's very kind.

You should go.

She should?

I should?!

She is an American girl. That's what they do.

Wait until A-má sees our new Cici.

I AM an American girl.

Chapter 22

Remember to act super surprised when we bring A-má.

Yes, Cici.

Maybe she missed her flight.

I don't see A-má.

Why's it taking so long?

Did she really get on the plane?

n, Terry, and Schuyler—L.L.M.

To friends who kept me uplifted
and encouraged every step of the way—A.X.

HarperAlley is an imprint of HarperCollins Publishers.

Measuring Up
Text copyright © 2020 by Lily LaMotte
Illustrations copyright © 2020 by Ann Xu
Colors by Sunmi. Flats by Cynthia Yuan Cheng and Ashanti Fortson.
All rights reserved. Printed in Bosnia and Herzegovina.

Library of Congress Control Number: 2020938942
ISBN 978-0-06-297387-0 — ISBN 978-0-06-297386-3 (pbk.)

The artist used ink on paper and Adobe Photoshop to create the digital illustrations for this book.
Typography by Erica De Chavez
21 22 23 24   GPS   10 9 8 7 6 5
❖
First Edition